Earthquake!

Earthquake!

Jules Archer

A LUCAS·EVANS BOOK

CRESTWOOD HOUSE
New York
Collier Macmillan Canada
Toronto
Maxwell Macmillan International Publishing Group
New York   Oxford   Singapore   Sydney

*For my grandchildren: Zachary, Nathaniel,
Cameron, Kirsten, Roy, Ryan, Colleen and Erin*

COVER: Geologist Jim Berkland stands neck-deep in a huge fissure created by the
California earthquake of October 1989.
FRONTIS: In August 1959 a fence along Montana State Highway 499 buckled when an
earthquake depressed the ground on one side.
PAGE 7: The great Alaska earthquake of March 27, 1964, caused a landslide in
Anchorage that tore apart an elementary school and turned the schoolyard
into this jumble.

PHOTO CREDITS: *Cover*, Shmuel Thaler, *Santa Cruz Sentinel*; *Frontis*, I. J. Witkind, U.S. Geo-
logical Survey Photo Library; *Page 7*, U.S. Geological Survey Photo Library; *Page 8*, Bill Lovejoy,
Santa Cruz Sentinel; *Page 16*, W. C. Mendenhall, U.S. Geological Survey Photo Library; *Page
17*, U.S. Geological Survey Photo Library; *Page 18*, I. J. Witkind, U.S. Geological Survey Photo
Library; *Pages 20, 21*, Henry Helbush, NOAA; *Page 22*, U.S. Geological Survey Photo Library;
Page 24, M. Celebi, U.S. Geological Survey Photo Library; *Pages 26–27*, Shmuel Thaler, *Santa
Cruz Sentinel*; *Page 29*, J. K. Hillers, U.S. Geological Survey Photo Library; *Page 30*, M. Celebi,
U.S. Geological Survey Photo Library; *Page 31*, R. Kachadoorian, U.S. Geological Survey Photo
Library; *Pages 32–33*, U.S. Geological Survey Photo Library; *Page 35*, U.S. Geological Survey
Photo Library; *Page 36*, R. Kachadoorian, U.S. Geological Survey Photo Library; *Page 37*, U.S.
Geological Survey Photo Library; *Page 39*, U.S. Geological Survey Photo Library; *Pages 40–41*,
R. Kachadoorian, U.S. Geological Survey Photo Library; *Page 42*, Mrs. Harry A. Simms, Sr.

BOOK DESIGN: Barbara DuPree Knowles   DIAGRAMS: Andrew Edwards

LIBRARY OF CONGRESS CATALOGING-IN-PUBLICATION DATA

Archer, Jules.
    Earthquake! / by Jules Archer.—1st ed.
    p.   cm. — (Nature's disasters)
    SUMMARY: Examines the nature, origins, and dangers of earthquakes and discusses the
warning system that predicts and detects them.
    ISBN 0-89686-593-2
    1. Earthquakes—Juvenile literature. [1.Earthquakes]   I. Title. II. Series.
    QE521.3.A73   1991   551.2′2—dc20   90-45370

Crestwood House   Collier Macmillan Canada, Inc.
Macmillan Publishing Company   1200 Eglinton Avenue East
866 Third Avenue   Suite 200
New York, NY 10022   Don Mills, Ontario M3C 3N1
                              First Edition

Printed in the United States of America   10 9 8 7 6 5 4 3 2 1

Contents

Earthquake!

Sleeping in a tent on a small south-west Pacific Island, I suddenly woke one night when something shook me violently. To my amazement, my cot was jumping up and down. I heard a terrible noise, like thunder magnified a hundred times.

In my fright I sprang from my cot and grabbed on to the tent pole. To my horror the pole jerked me up and down. I dashed out of my tent into our jungle clearing. The ground was jumping under my feet—huge jumps, almost a foot each time. I staggered to the nearest coconut tree and held on for dear life. But the tree was also jumping. Coconuts shaken loose thudded around me.

There was nothing solidly fixed to which I could cling. The ground kept jumping under my feet. Roaring noises made it seem as if the earth were shaking apart.

I can't remember now just how long the **earthquake** lasted. The time was probably less than a minute. But each second seemed like an endless hour of pure panic. My guess is that the earthquake reached 8.0 on the **Richter scale.** A 9.0 is the measurement of the worst earthquake possible.

The catastrophic earthquake in northern California in October 1989 brought President George Bush to Santa Cruz to examine the damage.

The next big earthquake I experienced took place in Santa Cruz, California. The date was Tuesday, October 17, 1989; the time, 5:04 P.M. Suddenly the floor began to shake violently. There was a tremendous roaring noise. The kitchen cupboards flew open. Dishes, glasses and jars crashed around us. Appliances shook off the counters. A vine-laden trellis fell over onto the dinette table. A long cement-block bookcase in the living room crashed onto the floor, jumbling my books. Everything loose in my office flew into a scrambled mess. Pictures jumped off the walls.

Elsewhere in Santa Cruz one man was thrown straight up in the air, flipped 180 degrees, and landed on his head. In a house nearby, a refrigerator broke loose, smashed against the opposite wall, then crashed back again.

The quake lasted 15 long seconds—the largest California quake in 37 years. It raised the San Andreas Fault four feet farther north toward San Francisco.

Four people in town were crushed to death by falling brick walls. Mountain area houses were knocked off their foundations. Fifty homes were destroyed, shaken to pieces or set on fire. City officials estimated the damage to homeowners at $70 million. In the Santa Cruz Mall, almost all the stores and buildings were damaged beyond repair. They had to be demolished.

The quake measured 7.1 on the Richter scale. Thousands of frightened people refused to sleep in their homes that night. Many slept out in their gardens or cars for a whole week. Ninety aftershocks continued to rock Santa Cruz County for an entire month. Severe landslides closed essential highways.

The earthquake was so mighty that it shook San Francisco and Oakland 70 miles north. It collapsed bridges there, trapping people in cars and killing over 60. Much of a San Francisco neighborhood called the Marina was destroyed.

Northern Californians were severely shaken by the disaster. Some fled the beautiful state, unwilling to risk another quake. And more quakes will come—no doubt about it. California is earthquake country, situated over many great earth faults. Another major quake may erupt tomorrow. Or in 30 years. No one knows when.

WHY EARTHQUAKES OCCUR

Our Drifting Continents

The land above the earth's oceans consists of seven continents—North America, South America, Europe, Asia, Africa, Australia and Antarctica. The first maps of the world were drawn in the early 17th century. English scholar Francis Bacon noticed something peculiar about them. If the continents could be fit together like parts of a jigsaw puzzle, their coastlines would match each other.

In 1912 that idea led German **meteorologist** Alfred Wegener to an important **theory.** He surmised that about 200 million years ago the continents *were* all connected. He believed they formed just one huge landmass, which lay half above and half below the equator. Today most of the earth's land lies above the equator, in the Northern Hemisphere. Wegener's theory was later supported by **paleontologists** who found similar **fossils** on every continent. There was no way these prehistoric creatures could have crossed the oceans from continent to continent.

But why did the continents long ago break away from the one big landmass? And how did they drift to their world positions today?

The inside of the earth is divided into three parts: the **mantle,** which lies just beneath the crust; the outer core; and the inner core. The **crust** is the earth's "skin."

Earth scientists believe that our continents and ocean floors are masses of granite. They ride on heavier, 70-mile-thick blocks of the earth's crust. These blocks are called **tectonic plates.** They bump into and slide past each other like huge ice floes. They drift slowly around on a hot, soft zone within the earth's mantle called the **asthenosphere.** Carrying the continents with them, the plates move as much as four inches a year. They drifted that way for hundreds of millions of years until there were big distances between the continents.

But what causes these plates to keep moving? How and why did they break the ancient single landmass into seven continents?

Earth Plates Move Around

Like people jammed in a subway, the plates crowd each other, drifting edge to edge. Upwelling thermal currents in the asthenosphere shove the plates apart in some places. As this happens, more distant plates are pushed together.

Continental drift results where major plates are slowly but steadily shoved apart. They carry the continents with them. Wherever plates collide slowly, their edges crumple like wrinkling rugs. That is how mountain ranges are formed, either on land or under the ocean.

One plate may move faster than one blocking its path. The slower plate usually slips beneath the faster one down into the mantle. The mantle's fierce heat melts all or part of it. The plate doesn't carry its piggybacking continent down with it because continents are made of lighter rock.

The earth's crust consists of separated, 70-mile-thick tectonic plates that bump into and slide past each other like huge blocks of ice.

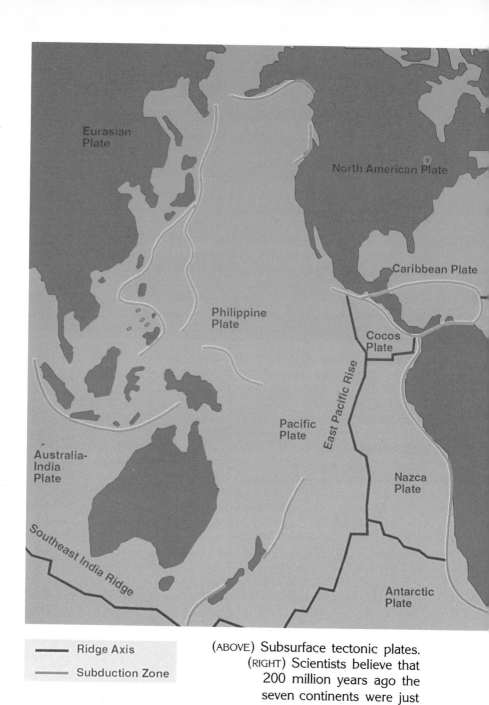

Eurasian Plate

North American Plate

Caribbean Plate

Philippine Plate

Cocos Plate

East Pacific Rise

Pacific Plate

Australia-India Plate

Nazca Plate

Southeast India Ridge

Antarctic Plate

——— Ridge Axis

~~~~~ Subduction Zone

(ABOVE) Subsurface tectonic plates.
(RIGHT) Scientists believe that
200 million years ago the
seven continents were just
one huge landmass.

12

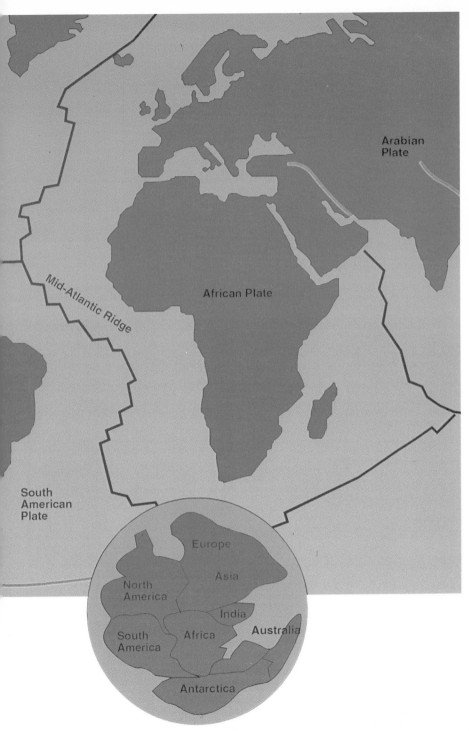

Arabian Plate

Mid-Atlantic Ridge

African Plate

South American Plate

Europe

Asia

North America

India

South America

Africa

Australia

Antarctica

13

But what causes the upwelling hot currents that force the plates to keep moving? Basically, it's the heat of the earth's inner and outer cores and the mantle. The constantly boiling currents they produce operate much like boiling water. Their upward thrust pressures the plates to shift position.

WHAT IS
AN EARTHQUAKE?

Regions with high mountains, especially those near deep seas, are most likely to experience earthquakes.

Almost all quakes take place in one of two great earthquake-prone belts. The first belt runs along the coastlines bordering the Pacific Ocean. This includes Chile in South America; north to the coast of the United States and Alaska; west along the Aleutian Islands; and south through Japan, the Philippines and the East Indies. This belt is often called the **Ring of Fire** because it also contains active volcanoes. Four out of five of the world's quakes occur in the Ring of Fire.

The second earthquake belt runs from Southeast Asia through the Mediterranean and out into the Atlantic Ocean.

What Are Earthquake Faults?

Faults are great fractures between masses of rock at the earth's surface. They mark the boundaries where two tectonic plates meet or try to pass. When the pressures between two opposing plates become so great that they break the earth's crust, earthquakes occur along these faults. Most faults lie beneath the earth's surface, but some are visible as long trenches in the ground.

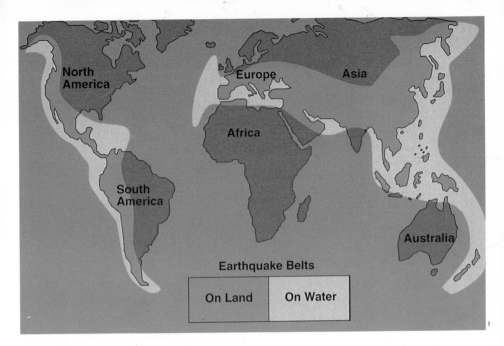

Almost all earthquakes take place in one of two great earthquake belts.

The most famous fault is the San Andreas Fault, which runs parallel to the coast of California. It stretches 700 miles long. The 1906 quake that devastated San Francisco took place along this fault. The plate on the ocean side of the fault is pressing steadily northward against the eastern-side plate at a rate of two inches a year. In a few million years the city of Los Angeles may have ridden up to where San Francisco now stands!

An earthquake's **shock waves** traveling along the surface of a fault usually rupture everything in their path. They can rip houses in half and crumble bridges. Major faults also have several smaller fault branches that can shake, rattle and roll. A quake often shifts the sides of a fault. The ground on one side may move forward and upward by several feet, and backward and downward on the other.

15

San Francisco after the famous earthquake of 1906.

What Are the Different Ways
Earthquakes Strike?

When two plates moving in different directions block each other's path along a fault, pressures build up. The grinding and rubbing of rock against rock sets up earth tremors. Each plate tries to push past or above the other. The stress may become too great, and then something gives way violently. The site of this violent movement beneath the earth is called the **focus** of the quake.

The sudden shift of these great rock masses sends shock waves through the globe. These may last only a few seconds. The result, however, can be a terrible killer quake. Damage can spread great distances from the **epicenter,** the point on the earth's surface above the focus.

The intensity of an earthquake varies with its size. It may be so minor as to be scarcely felt at its epicenter. Or heavy vibrations may shake hundreds of thousands of square miles.

Those who live in earthquake zones are safer when plates move very slowly past each other with only frequent, small tremors. That's because the energy created by the opposing plates is released gradually. There is greater danger when the plates snag. Their constantly building pressure causes one of the locked giants to tear loose violently. The result is a huge shock and a big earthquake.

Shock waves radiate out from the epicenter faster than a bullet. Primary waves travel along the surface, pushing upward everything in their path. Secondary waves, or **shear waves,** rock from side to side about two miles a second.

Before the 1964 Alaskan earthquake, the sidewalk in downtown Anchorage in front of the stores on the right was at a level with the street on the left.

During a 1959 earthquake in Montana, many stone chimneys crashed into pieces. But the log cabins, like the one shown above, were usually undamaged. Buildings made of wood have more flexibility than those made of brick or stone. So they can better survive an earthquake.

They shake everything in their path, the way a dog might shake loose a rag from its master's hand.

Seismographs—instruments that record these waves—are stationed at different places throughout the world. This lets scientists pinpoint both the focus and epicenter of an earthquake.

Why Do We Have Aftershocks?

Almost every major quake is followed by a series of smaller shakes. These may occur hours, days, weeks or months afterward. As a rule, with time they grow less in size and frequency.

These **aftershocks** occur even though the major strain between two plates is released by an earthquake. The plates' touching edges still have to readjust to new positions. These edges may not be able to pass each other smoothly. Thus smaller shocks result.

Aftershocks can also do serious damage. They can shake down buildings, roads and bridges already weakened by the main quake. They frighten people rattled by the earthquake, making them worry that another big quake may be about to occur.

Tsunamis—Great Walls of Rolling Water

When an earthquake occurs under the sea, it is called a seaquake. The energy waves that are created can travel along the ocean floor at speeds of up to 500 miles an hour. They produce towering surface waves known by their Japanese name, **tsunamis.** They are also called tidal waves. These waves can also be set in motion by coastal land earthquakes.

Tsunamis most commonly occur in the Pacific and Indian oceans. Coasts with beaches that gradually step down are most vulnerable. The great force of a tsunami piles up a huge wave crest in an enormous wall of water often over 100 feet high. Crashing inland, it can drown and sweep away everything in its path. It often floods the coastal region.

One tsunami in the Yaeyama Islands, off Taiwan, rose to 260 feet high. It drowned 11,000 people. In 1896 a Japanese tsunami killed 27,000 people. It washed away 10,000 homes and 7,000 fishing boats. A huge tsunami hit Port Royal, Jamaica, in 1692. It lifted a large English frigate and carried it clear over the town to the port on the other side. Some people struggling in the water managed to grab the ship's cables and pulled themselves aboard. They rode to safety above the housetops!

(ABOVE AND OPPOSITE PAGE) The progress of a tsunami. Caused by an earthquake in 1957 near Alaska, the 26-foot-high wave hit Oahu Island, Hawaii, 2,235 miles away.

Strangely, the first sign of an approaching tsunami is the sea tide ebbing drastically from the shore. The sea bottom is exposed for some distance out. Then the ocean tide flows back in again, higher and faster. These changes may be repeated several times before the full force of the tsunami roars in.

Its towering wall of water can crash inland with the weight of millions of tons. In his book *Earthquakes*, **seismologist** Nicholas Heck wrote in awe, "It is the most spectacular and appalling of all earthquake phenomena."

Aftermath of a tsunami on Kodiak Island, Alaska, following the 1964 quake.

The first earthquake shock waves that roared under Anchorage, Alaska, in 1964, created tsunamis. They sped along the Pacific coast at over 400 miles an hour. Seven hours later they hit Crescent City, California. Ten people drowned and 150 stores were smashed. Other tsunamis traveled 4,000 miles from Alaska to crash into Japan.

The U.S. Coast and Geodetic Survey (USCGS) operates a tidal-wave warning service in the Pacific area. Seismograph stations locate the position of an earthquake. The USCGS then calculates the time of arrival of expected tsunamis. Thus, warning can be issued hours in advance. That gives people living in threatened areas time to evacuate to higher ground.

Strange Earthquake Sights

Primary earthquake waves can send large rocks jumping into the air. During an 1837 earthquake in Chile, a ship's mast that had been sunk 30 feet under the sea suddenly rose above the surface. In a 1923 earthquake in Japan, wells jumped 10 feet out of the ground. Oak trees in an 1811 quake in Missouri split 40 feet up their trunks, half left on either side of the fault.

America's most famous earthquake occurred in San Francisco in 1906. It damaged towns north and south for a distance of 300 miles and was felt as far south as Mexico. A police sergeant reported, "The whole street was undulating. It was as if the waves of the ocean were coming toward me."

In a 40-second shock, buildings jumped, towers fell, bridges twisted, and houses split apart. After 10 seconds, another 25-second shock hit. Streets rose and fell. Buildings collapsed. Gas mains erupted. Then fires broke out all over the city. Fire engines seeking to fight the blazes found all the water mains broken. San Francisco burned for almost four days, gutting the city. The death toll was 600.

Two weeks after a 1931 quake in New Zealand, two acres of rocks suddenly rose seven feet out of the sea at Tuamotu Island, hundreds of miles off the New Zealand coast. During a 1948 quake in Japan, a woman was hurled into a fault. She was buried up to her neck by falling earth, which crushed her to death.

In the 1964 quake in Alaska, a tsunami swept huge locomotives and loaded freight cars off their tracks. It flung them into the city streets of Seward. In the same year, a quake in Japan caused an island to rise five feet in a series of surges.

The top floors of these buildings in Mexico City collapsed during the September 1985 quake.

CAN EARTHQUAKES BE PREDICTED?

Is there a way to tell when an earthquake is coming? For one thing, more quakes generally occur in the winter than in the summer. Often there is a surge of unusually warm weather. Some evidence suggests that quakes are more likely to occur when the moon is closest to the earth. The moon's **gravitational pull,** which causes tides, may also affect the earth's plates. Another theory suggests that in years when sun flares reach great heights, the earth is shaken by solar winds.

Some earth changes may foreshadow a large quake. One side of a fault may rise up a bit. Small earth tremors may be felt. Water may seep up from the earth. The level of well water may shift noticeably. These are not surefire indications, however. Many earthquakes occur suddenly, without warning.

Can Animals Predict Earthquakes?

One might also observe the behavior of animals. There is some evidence that they sense approaching quakes early on. Horses have been known to rear and race away before a quake strikes. The Japanese pay attention to pheasants, which scream as if alarmed before a quake. Dogs howled all night before the 1906 San Francisco quake. Fish have jumped out of the water. Pet cats have run away. Snakes and rats have come out of their hiding places.

Before the 1835 quake in Chile, all dogs in the city of Talcahuano raced out of town. Horses kicked at their stalls trying to get loose just before an 1887 quake. An approaching 1954 quake in Greece was signaled by storks flying off

This photo was taken on October 18, 1989,
the day after the devastating earthquake in Santa Cruz,

California, and shows the heavy damage inflicted
on the downtown Pacific Garden Mall.

in an agitated manner. Villagers observing this saved their lives by fleeing their homes for open spaces.

In China in 1975 the Geological Bureau of Beijing reported that 58 species of wild and domestic animals had noticeable behavior reactions before earthquakes. Chickens, for example, flew up in trees and screeched loudly. Cats picked their kittens up in their mouths and ran.

Where Can Big Earthquakes Be Expected?

Usually once a region has suffered a major quake—measuring 7.0 or more—it is likely to be free of other major quakes for at least several decades. That's because the great stress of conflicting plates below the earth's surface has been relieved. But the longer an area along a fault in an earthquake belt has gone without a major quake, the more likely one is to occur.

Scientists know which areas will be struck. But they aren't certain just when the earthquakes will erupt. In 1977 Congress passed the National Earthquake Hazard Reduction Program Act. This provides funds to U.S. scientific agencies so that they can do constant research. More accurate predictions, therefore, are possible in time to save lives and property.

The Pacific Tsunami Warning Center in Hawaii monitors all earthquakes to determine their location and size. When these are likely to generate tsunamis, all Pacific nations are alerted. If tsunami waves are actually detected, the alerts become warnings. This allows countries at risk to take precautions.

China's scientists also do research on earthquake prediction. A program involving 10,000 amateur workers has been able to issue timely warnings for about ten major quakes.

Ninety percent of American earthquakes take place on the West Coast. A major quake *could* occur anywhere, however, in the United States. In 1884 one severe quake hit Jamaica, Queens, only 15 miles from Manhattan.

Robert Ketter is director of the National Center for Earthquake Engineering Research. He considers it probable that a major quake will hit the eastern seaboard before the year 2010. Devastation could be terrible, because few eastern cities have California's building codes, which require anti-earthquake construction.

Scientists have to be careful not to issue quake predictions too often. Quake warnings disrupt business, keep tourists away and alarm the population. A predicted quake may fail to occur within a reasonable time span. Then people may simply stop paying attention to the scientists' warnings.

Earthquake wreckage in Charleston, South Carolina, August 1886.

The top four floors of this building in Mexico City collapsed when the 1985 quake pounded them against the next building.

EARTHQUAKE DAMAGE

How much damage an earthquake causes depends chiefly on the area hit. If a major quake strikes a territory that is largely unpopulated, it causes low loss of life or property. But if it hits a crowded city, there may be many deaths, injuries and destruction.

An earthquake that hit Los Angeles a century ago would have troubled some 100,000 people. Today it would affect over a million out of that city's current population of 3 million. Many areas in California that were sparsely populated early in the century are now industrial centers.

Even this highway support of steel-reinforced concrete could not withstand the shaking of a 1971 California quake.

The 1964 Alaska earthquake pushed part of this railroad bridge into the Copper River.

Some of these are covered with great housing developments. Obviously, major earthquakes hitting those areas today could do terrible damage.

Most cities around the world have at least tripled their populations in the last one hundred years. Major quakes could tumble their skyscrapers, factories and power plants. They could rock millions of people with tremendous shock waves.

An earthquake can also create havoc by breaking underground water and gas pipes. Ruptured gas lines may set homes on fire. Broken water mains often make it difficult to put out such fires.

A quake can uproot trees and send them crashing over nearby homes. It can start landslides and avalanches. Masses of water can be sent surging out of lakes, rivers and dams.

Tall modern buildings sustain the least damage when they are directly at the epicenter. This is because they are best able to withstand the up-and-down shaking of primary waves. On the other hand, the snakelike shear waves occur some distance from the epicenter. They cause the greatest stress by shaking buildings from side to side. Often these are knocked off their foundations.

Buildings with thick, heavy walls are unable to resist these waves. Violent quakes often shake them down and bury people within. Brick buildings are the most vulnerable. Chimneys and heavy roof tiles are frequently shaken off. They can crash onto people standing or passing below.

Homes and districts built on soft or filled-in soil suffer most. They feel the force of the shock waves most directly. As a rule, those built on bedrock suffer less damage.

Fires and floods often do the greatest damage in quakes. The major destruction in the 1906 San Francisco quake was caused by the fires that followed.

A quake can also break dams high in the mountains above a city or valley. Floods can then sweep down and drown everything in their path.

A quake that lasts less than 60 seconds can cause devastation that will plague its victims for many years to come. A series of severe earthquakes shook Managua, Nicaragua, in 1972. Fifteen years later, the torn-up city still looked as though an earthquake had just occurred the week before. The impoverished country lacked the money to rebuild.

A six-story apartment house in Anchorage felled by the great 1964 Alaskan earthquake. The elevator shaft and stairwell toppled and came to rest on the rubble.

This San Fernando, California, house shifted 10 to 12 feet off its foundation during the February 1971 quake.

HOW TO BEHAVE
DURING A BIG EARTHQUAKE

What should you do when the floor of your living room begins to sway like a rolling ship at sea? When the furniture starts jumping around?

First of all, try to stay calm. Quickly duck under a desk or table, or into a doorway. Or roll under a bed. Keep away from windows, brick chimneys or anything that might fall over.

If outdoors, head for an open area. Stay away from trees, buildings, chimneys, walls and power lines. If you're in a downtown building, stay there. Get into a doorway if possible. It is a strong support in a building. If you're in a car, pull over to the side of the road and stop. Overpasses, bridges and power lines should be avoided. Stay inside until the shaking is over. Be prepared for aftershocks. When the major quake stops, get to open ground quickly.

What to Do After a Quake

Check yourself and your family and neighbors for injuries. Help with first aid where needed or phone for a doctor. Check for fires. Inspect for gas and water leaks. Know

A 1906 Alaskan earthquake tore apart this approach to a railroad bridge. It put a hump in the bridge too.

where main valves are and, if necessary, shut them off. The front of your phone book might tell you how. If a gas smell persists, open the windows and phone the gas company. Then leave the building.

Keep a supply of fresh batteries handy for a battery-operated radio in case the electricity fails. Turn on a radio or TV for emergency bulletins and information. Check food and water supplies. Don't eat or drink anything from open containers near shattered glass. If possible, fill big bottles and the bathtub with water, in case a water main breaks. Don't flush the toilet if the water is shut off. Check your house for cracks and damage. Stay off the streets so that emergency workers can get through. Use the phone only for emergency calls.

Preparing for Earthquakes

The U.S. Geological Survey's National Earthquake Information Service is in Golden, Colorado. The service collects information from 3,000 seismological stations in some 125 countries. But earthquake prediction is still in its experimental stages.

In earthquake country, being prepared is the safest course. It isn't a question of *if* quakes will occur, but only *when.*

Water heaters, cabinets, bookcases, shelves and plants should be fastened to the wall to resist earth tremors. Cabinets and china cupboards should be latched so that the doors stay closed. Heavy items and breakables in closets and cupboards should be stored on lower shelves. Each family member should know the safest place to stand or crouch if a quake strikes. Each should know how to shut off the switches that control electricity, gas and water.

A landslide caused this theater marquee in Anchorage, Alaska, to drop 11 feet to the sidewalk during the 1964 quake.

You should have enough drinking water and canned food stored in your house for a few days. Items that you can reach easily should include flashlights with spare batteries, water purification tablets, a battery-operated radio, a fire extinguisher and first-aid supplies.

People are safest in areas where government authorities require houses, buildings, roads and bridges, both old and new, to pass inspection by seismologist engineers.

When the 1989 Santa Cruz quake rocked San Francisco, the city's many skyscrapers shook and swayed, but they did not fall.

Aerial view of a collapsed highway overpass in

San Fernando, California, after the 1971 quake.

Two views of the tsunami that began in the Aleutian Islands off Alaska in 1946 and traveled more than 2,000 miles to the shores of the Hawaiian Islands. Waves ranged from 20 to 55 feet high!

This was because the city's building codes required better bolting down of the skyscrapers' understructures. Earthquake resistance was also helped by the use of reinforced concrete, which kept its strength because it was made to withstand movement.

The quake did kill over 60 people when a road collapsed onto another one below it. But the California quake measured the same as a quake the previous year in Armenia that killed 25,000 people living in poorly constructed buildings. Half a million Armenians were left homeless.

CAN EARTHQUAKES BE TAMED?

Some scientists are thinking about ways to reduce the power of earthquakes. They suggest making the tectonic plates drift past each other more smoothly. Their idea is to lubricate areas of the crust by drilling deep wells into the faults and pumping water down.

This might make the edges of the plates slippery enough to allow them to move past each other more easily. If that worked, there would be no building up of the great pressures that cause earthquakes. Instead, there might be, at worst, only some tremors. These would do a lot less damage and kill a lot fewer people.

But that possibility lies far in the future. Scientists have come a long way in understanding what causes earthquakes. In fact, scientific advances have given us more control over the elements than, perhaps, our ancestors could ever have imagined. But we still have a lot to learn before we can tame earthquakes—one of the most terrifying of nature's disasters.

Some Famous

1556   Shensi, China: The deadliest earthquake of all time kills 830,000 people.

1755   Lisbon, Portugal: The city is drowned by a 50-foot-high tsunami in a quake that kills 60,000.

1811–
1812   New Madrid, Missouri: Quakes open up earth cracks to five miles long, ten feet wide and five feet deep.

1891   Central Japan: A quake crumbles almost every building. Whole forests slip down mountains into valleys.

1899   Displacement Bay, Alaska: Aptly named. A quake lifts a flat beach onto a cliff almost 50 feet high.

1906   San Francisco, California: In America's most famous quake, buildings jump and collapse. Towers fall. Bridges twist. Fires blaze for almost four days. Death toll: 600.

1908   Calabria, Italy: Following a quake, a four-story-high tsunami crushes and drowns almost 100,000 Italians.

1923   Tokyo and Yokohama, Japan: Both cities burn for two days after an 8.3 quake. Over 150,000 Japanese perish.

1939   Chile: One of that country's worst quakes kills 28,000 and leaves 700,000 homeless.

1960   Chile: An 8.3 quake raises 24-foot-high walls of water that sweep away entire fishing villages. Death toll: 5,000.

Earthquakes

1963   Skopje, Yugoslavia. Over 1,100 die when a nighttime quake sends people screaming into the streets in pajamas and nightgowns.

1964   Alaska: An 8.5 quake shakes a million square miles. Anchorage buildings and pavements sink up to 30 feet. Three-fourths of all factories collapse. A tsunami carrying flaming oil crushes and burns homes.

1971   Peru: A quake breaks a great mass of ice and rock loose from a glacier. Crushed dead: 50,000. Homeless: 80,000.

1976   Tangshan, China: A quake kills 242,000 people.

1990   Iran: A devastating quake kills up to 50,000 people and injures over 60,000. Whole villages are reduced to ruins, with tens of thousands buried under rubble.

Glossary

asthenosphere The hot top part of the earth's mantle, just under the crust.

aftershocks Smaller quakes that follow a major earthquake.

continental drift The breakup of the earth's original single landmass into continents that then separated.

crust The outside solid part of the earth's surface.

earthquake A vibration or trembling of the ground caused by movement of the subsurface.

epicenter The point on the earth's surface directly above the focus of the quake.

faults Great splits between masses of rock at the earth's surface.

focus The point where the earthquake begins below the earth's surface.

fossil The impression of an ancient animal or plant left in a rock deposit, or the animal or plant itself.

gravitational pull The force that draws all bodies in the universe toward one another.

mantle Fiercely hot rock 1,800 miles deep beneath the crust.

meteorologist A scientist who studies or forecasts weather variations.

paleontologist A scientist who studies fossils to determine facts about prehistoric plants and creatures.

Richter scale The system invented by Dr. Charles F. Richter to measure the strength of earthquakes.

Ring of Fire The earthquake and volcano belt in countries that rim the Pacific Ocean.

seismographs Instruments that make an automatic record of the time, duration, direction and intensity of earthquakes.

seismologist A scientist who studies earthquakes and their causes and results.

shear waves Waves that radiate out from an earthquake's epicenter rocking from side to side at a fast pace.

shock waves Earthquake waves that travel along the surface with a swift up-and-down motion.

tectonic plates 70-mile-thick blocks of the earth's crust on which the continents ride.
theory A belief explaining something, backed by certain facts.
tsunami A towering ocean wave set in motion by either seaquakes or coastal land earthquakes.

For Further Reading

Asimov, Isaac. *How Did We Find Out about Earthquakes?* New York: Walker and Company, 1978.

Cazeau, Charles. *Earthquakes*. Chicago: Follett Publishing Co., 1974.

Christopher, Matt. *Earthquake*. Boston: Little, Brown & Co., 1975.

Halacy, D. S. *Earthquakes: A Natural History*. New York: Bobbs-Merrill Co., 1974.

Lauber, Patricia. *Earthquakes: New Scientific Ideas about How & Why the Earth Shakes*. New York: Random House, Inc., 1972.

Paananen, Eloise. *Tremor! Earthquake Technology in the Space Age*. New York: Julian Messner, 1982.

Tributsch, Helmut. *When the Snakes Awake*. Cambridge, Mass.: The MIT Press, 1982.

INDEX